# COCK A DOODLE-DOO, MR SULTANA!

Also by Michael Morpurgo and Shoo Rayner:

Cock-a-doodle-doo!

Alien Invasion!

Pigs Might Fly!

Other titles by Michael Morpurgo:

Mr Skip

The Butterfly Lion

Dear Olly

Toro! Toro!

Cool!

Born to Run

# michael morpurgo

## COCKADOODLE-DOO, MR SULTANA!

Illustrated by Shoo Rayner

HarperCollins *Children's Books*

First published in Great Britain by Scholastic Ltd in 1998
Published by HarperCollins *Children's Books* in 2012
HarperCollins *Children's Books* is a division of HarperCollins*Publishers* Ltd,
77-85 Fulham Palace Road, Hammersmith, London, W6 8JB
This edition published by HarperCollins *Children's Books* in 2013

The HarperCollins website address is: www.harpercollins.co.uk

1

Text copyright © Michael Morpurgo 1998
Illustration copyright © Shoo Rayner 2012

ISBN 978-0-00-748998-5

Michael Morpurgo and Shoo Rayner assert the moral right
to be identified as the author and illustrator of the work.
All rights reserved.

Printed and bound in England by Clays Ltd, St Ives plc

MIX
Paper from
responsible sources
FSC   FSC C007454
www.fsc.org

FSC™ is a non-profit international organisation established to promote
the responsible management of the world's forests. Products carrying the
FSC label are independently certified to assure consumers that they come
from forests that are managed to meet the social, economic and
ecological needs of present and future generations,
and other controlled sources.

Find out more about HarperCollins and the environment at
www.harpercollins.co.uk/green

# The Greedy Sultan

In a far-off Eastern land, a long, long time ago, there once lived a great and **mighty** Sultan. He was, without doubt, the richest, laziest, greediest and **fattest** Sultan there had ever been.

He was so rich his palace was
built of nothing but shining
marble and glowing gold, so

rich that even the buttons on his silken clothes were made of diamonds.

He was so **lazy** he had to have a special servant to brush his teeth for him, and another one to dress him.

# The Greedy Sultan

He did nothing for himself, except eat. He was so **greedy** that every meal — breakfast, lunch and dinner — he'd gobble down a nice plump peacock just to himself, and a great bowl of sweetmeats, too.

And then he'd wash it all down with a jug of honeyed camel's milk.

It was because he was so very **lazy** and SO very greedy that he was so very, very **fat.**

He had to sleep in a bed

**wide**

enough for five grown men,

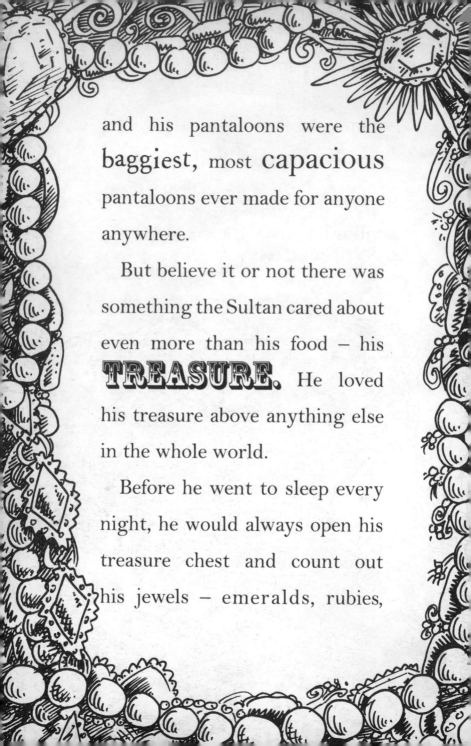

and his pantaloons were the **baggiest,** most **capacious** pantaloons ever made for anyone anywhere.

But believe it or not there was something the Sultan cared about even more than his food — his **TREASURE.** He loved his treasure above anything else in the whole world.

Before he went to sleep every night, he would always open his treasure chest and count out his jewels — emeralds, rubies, diamonds, pearls, sapphires, hundreds and hundreds of them — just to be quite sure they were all still there. Only then could he go to bed happy and sleep soundly.

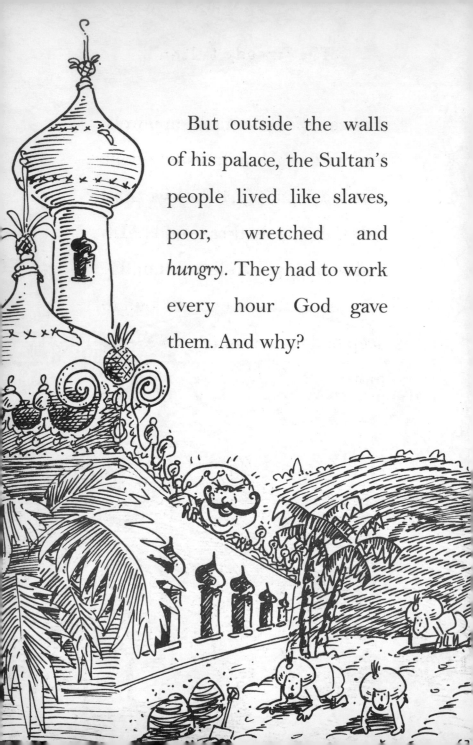

But outside the walls of his palace, the Sultan's people lived like slaves, poor, wretched and *hungry*. They had to work every hour God gave them. And why?

# The Greedy Sultan

To keep the Sultan rich in jewels.
Everything they harvested – their
corn, their grapes, their figs, their
dates, their pomegranates – ALL
had to be given to the Sultan. He
allowed them just enough food to
keep body and soul together – no
more.

# A Stumble
# on the Road

One fine morning, the Sultan was out hunting. He loved to hunt, because all he had to do was sit astride his horse and send the hawks off to do the hunting. There was only one horse in the land strong enough to carry him, a great **stout** old warhorse. But strong though he was, to be sat on by the great **fat** Sultan for hour after hour under the hot, hot, sun, proved too much even for him.

# Cockadoodle-doo, Mr Sultana!

Lathered up and exhausted, the old warhorse **staggered** suddenly and stumbled, throwing the Sultan to the ground.

# A Stumble on the Road

It took ten servants to get him
to his feet and brush him down.
He wasn't badly hurt, just a bit
bumped and bruised, but he was
angry; very angry.

He ordered his servants to whip the old horse soundly, so that he wouldn't do it again. Then they all helped him back up on his horse, which took some time, of course; and off they went back to the palace.

# Dropped in
# the Dust

The Sultan didn't know it, not yet, and no more did anyone else, but he'd left something behind lying in the dirt on the

**dusty** farmyard track, something that had popped off his waistcoat when he'd fallen from his horse.

 It was a button, a shining, glittering "diamond" button. Just a little way off down the farmyard track, was a **tumbledown** farmhouse where there lived a poor old woman. She had little enough in this world – though she never complained of it – only a couple of nanny goats for her milk, a few hens for her eggs, *and* a little red rooster. She always kept the goats hidden away inside her house, and the hens too, for fear that the Sultan's servants might come by and steal them away for the Sultan.

She had always tried to keep her little red rooster in the house too, because she loved him dearly, and because she wanted him to keep her hens happy. But this was a little red rooster with a mind of his own, and whenever he could, he would go *running* off to explore the big, wide world outside, to find friends — and to find food, for he was always very hungry.

# Little Red Rooster

That same day, when the poor old woman went out to fetch the water for her goats and hens, the little red rooster scooted out from under her skirts. Before she could stop him he was out through the open door and running off down the farm track.

"Come back, Little Red Rooster!" cried the poor old woman. "Come back! If the Sultan finds you, he'll catch you and eat you up.

Come back!"

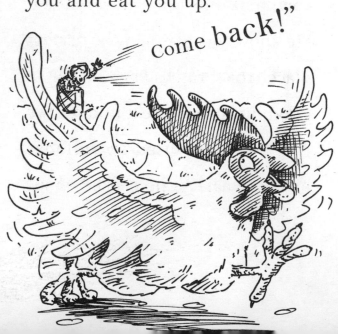

But the little red rooster had never in his life been frightened of anything or anyone. He just kept on running. "Catch me if you can, mistress mine," he called out.

On and on he ran, until he came to the farm track where the cornfield and the vineyard met. He knew this was just the perfect place to scratch around for a good meal. Here he'd find all the ripe corn and dried-up sultanas he could eat. As he pecked about busily in the earth, he came across dozens of *wriggling worms*

*and singing cicadas*

*and burrowing beetles,*

but he never ate these. After all, these were his friends. He couldn't eat his friends – though he had thought about it once or twice.

# A Horrible Temper

**M**eanwhile, back in his gold and marble palace, the great Sultan was stamping up and down. He was in a horrible temper, his stomachs and his chins **wobbling** with fury.

"The diamond button off my waistcoat," he **roared**. "I have lost my diamond button. Search, you miserable beggars, search everywhere, every nook and cranny."

His servants were scurrying here and there and everywhere, all over the palace, but they could not find it anywhere.

"I'll **LOP** off your heads if you don't find it," he bellowed. But no matter how loud he shouted, how terrible the threats, no one could find the missing diamond button.

"Am I surrounded by nothing but **FOOLS** and imbeciles?" he thundered. "I see I shall have to find it myself. We shall go back and search every inch of the ground we hunted over this morning. And you will go in front of me, all of you on your knees in

34

the dust where you belong, and search for my diamond button. Fetch me my horse."

He clapped his hands.

"At once. AT ONCE."

# Finders Keepers

Out in the countryside, the little red rooster was scratching around in the dusty farm track at the edge of the cornfield.

He scratched
and he scratched.
Suddenly there
was something
strange in the earth,
something different, something
very pretty that glistened
and shone and twinkled in the
sun. He tried eating it, but it
didn't taste very good. So he
dropped it. And then he had a
sudden and brilliant idea.

"I know," he said to himself.
"Poor old mistress mine loves

pretty things. She's always saying so, and she's got nothing pretty of her own. I'll take it home for her. Then she won't be cross with me for running away, will she?"

But just as he picked it up again, along the farm track came the great **fat** Sultan on his horse, and in front of him, dozens of his servants, all of them crawling on their hands and knees in the dirt.

Closer and closer they came. All at once they spotted the little red rooster *and* the diamond button too, glinting in his beak.

"There, my lord Sultan!" they cried. "LOOK! That little red rooster. He's got your diamond button."

"So that's what it is," the little

red rooster said to himself.

The great **fat** Sultan rode up, scattering his servants hither and thither as he came. "Little Red Rooster," he said from high up on his horse. "I see you have my diamond button. I am your great and mighty Sultan. Give it to me at once. It's valuable, very valuable. And it's **mine**."

"I don't think so, Mr Sultana," replied the little red rooster, who had never in his life been frightened of anyone or anything.

Finders keepers. If it's so valuable, then I'm going to give it to poor mistress mine. She needs it a lot more than you, I think. Sorry, Mr Sultana."

**"What!"** spluttered the Sultan. "Mr Sultana? How dare you speak to me like that? How dare you? Did you hear what that infernal bird called me? Fetch me that rooster. Fetch me my diamond button! Grab him! Grab that rooster!"

# Cockadoodle-doo, Mr Sultana!

There was a frightful kerfuffle
of dust and feathers …

and SQUAWKING,

as the Sultan's servants tried to grab the little red rooster.

Whatever they did, they just could not catch him. In the end, the little red rooster ran off into the cornfield. But although he'd escaped their clutches, he was very cross with himself, for in all the kerfuffle he had dropped the diamond button.

# Cockadoodle-doo, Mr Sultana!

One of the Sultan's servants found it lying in the dust and brought it back to the Sultan. The Sultan was delighted, of course, and all his servants were mightily relieved, too. Now, at least, none of them would have his head lopped off, not that day anyway.

But had the Sultan seen the last of the little red rooster? Not by any means. The little red rooster wasn't going to give up that easily – he wasn't like that. He followed the Sultan and his servants back to the palace. Then, in the middle of the night, as everyone slept, he flew up to the Sultan's window, perched on the window-ledge, took a deep breath and crowed, and crowed.

He let out the loudest, longest
# cockadoodle-doo
he'd ever doodled in all his life.

**"COCKADOODLE-DOO,
MR SULTANA,"** he crowed.

**"COCKADOODLE-DOO!"**

The Sultan tried to cover his
ears. It didn't work.

# "COCKADOODLE -DOO!"

The Sultan tried to bury his head in his pillow. It didn't work.

"Cockadoodle-doo, Mr Sultana! Give me back my diamond button."

By now the Sultan was in a TERRIBLE rage. He had had quite enough of this. He called in his servants. "Grab me that infernal bird," he cried. "I know what I'll do. I know. We'll throw him in the well and drown him. That should **shut him up,** and shut him up for good."

# Hide-and-Seek

All night long, the Sultan and his servants chased around the palace after the little red rooster. The little red rooster

had LOTS of fun. He played
hide-and-seek behind the
peacocks.

He **flew,**

he **hopped,**

he **ran.**

He **perched** on cornices,

on chandeliers,

on the Sultan's throne itself!

And that was where they finally caught him. One of the servants crept up behind and grabbed him by his tail feathers.

The little red rooster didn't really mind – he'd had enough of the game anyway. He wasn't at all frightened of water. He knew

what to do with water.
He wasn't worried.

**"Aha!"** cried
the exultant Sultan.
"We've got you now.
You've crowed your
very last doodle-doo."

"I don't think so, Mr
Sultana," said the little
red rooster. But the
Sultan took him by the
neck and DROPPED
him down the well.

It was a long **flutter** down, and of course it was a bit wet when he landed. But the little red rooster didn't mind. He simply said to himself: *"Come, my empty stomach. Come, my empty stomach and drink up all the water."*

# You Again!

It took a bit of time, but that's just what he did. He drank up all the water, every last drop of it. Up and out of the well he flew, up and away, until he reached the Sultan's window.

**"COCKADOODLE-DOO, MR SULTANA!"** he cried.

"Give me back my DIAMOND BUTTON!"

The Sultan could not believe his eyes. He could not believe his ears. **"What!"** he spluttered. "You again!"

He called his servants. **"Look!"** he shrieked. "Can't you see? That infernal bird is back. I know what I'll do. I know. We'll grab him and throw him into the fire. Let him burn." So the Sultan's servants rushed at the little red rooster and caught him.

**"Aha!"** cried the

exultant Sultan. "We've got you now. You've crowed your very last doodle-doo."

"I don't think so, Mr Sultana," said the little red rooster. But the Sultan took him by the neck and **threw** him on the fire.

He wasn't at all frightened of fire. He knew what to do with fire. He wasn't worried. He simply said to himself: "*Come, my full-up stomach. Come, my full-up stomach, let out all the water and put out all the fire.*"

# The Last
# Doodle-doo

It took a bit of time, but that's just what he did. He gushed out all the water and put out all the fire, every last spark of

it. And up he flew again to the
Sultan's window.

"COCKADOODLE-DOO,
MR SULTANA," he cried.

"Give me back my diamond button."

"What!" spluttered the Sultan. **"You again!"**

Now the Sultan was really mad. He was beside himself with fury. He called his servants again. "Look! That infernal bird is back. I know what I'll do this time. I know. We'll grab him and throw him into the beehive. Let the bees **sting** him." And the Sultan's servants rushed at the little red rooster and caught him.

## Cockadoodle-doo, Mr Sultana!

**"Aha!"** cried the exultant Sultan. "We've got you now. You've crowed your very last doodle-doo."

## The Last Doodle-doo

"I don't think so, Mr Sultana," said the little red rooster. But the Sultan took him by the neck and **threw** him into the beehive.

# Cockadoodle-doo, Mr Sultana!

The little red rooster wasn't at all frightened by the bees. He knew what to do with bees. He wasn't worried. As the bees buzzed angrily all around him he simply said to himself: *"Come, my empty stomach. Come, my empty stomach and eat up all the bees."*

# The Last Doodle-doo

And that's just what he did. He
**ATE** up all the bees, every last
one of them.

# The Rooster's Revenge

**B**ack in the palace, the Sultan was rubbing his hands with glee. He thought for sure he had seen the last of the little red rooster. But he hadn't, had he?

He was happily tucking into his lunch of roast peacock, when suddenly he heard this:

"COCKADOODLE-DOO, MR SULTANA!

Give me back my diamond button." The little red rooster

was back on the window-ledge.

**"What!"** spluttered the Sultan, his mouth full of peacock. "You again!"

Like a CRAZED camel, he was, like a VENGEFUL vulture, like a JIBBERING jackal. He stamped and stormed about the palace, shouting and screaming at his servants.

"Who will rid me of this infernal bird?" he cried. "Tell me. Tell me how to do it, or I'll **LOP** off your heads.

I will! I will!"

And the servants knew he meant it, too. So naturally they all thought about how they could get rid of the little red rooster. They thought very hard, very hard indeed.

"Hang him by the neck from the pomegranate tree, my lord Sultan," said one. But the Sultan shook his head.

"Lop off his head, my lord Sultan," said another.

"It's no good," wailed the

Sultan. "He'd only run around without it." And he sat down in deep despair on his cushions.

But then, just as he was sitting down,

he heard the cushions sighing and groaning underneath him. He was squashing them flat!

**"That's it!"** he cried, leaping to his feet. "I know what I'll do. I'll sit on him and flatten him. I'll **squash** him. I'll **squish** him. I'll obsquatulate him!"

From the window-ledge the little red rooster heard it all and smiled inside himself.

The Sultan's servants rushed at the little red rooster and

caught him.

**"Aha!"** cried the exultant Sultan. "We've got you now. You've crowed your very last doodle-doo."

"I don't think so, Mr Sultana," said the little red rooster. But the Sultan took the little red rooster by the neck, stuffed him down the back of his pantaloons and then sat down on him, hard, very hard indeed.

The little red rooster wasn't at all frightened of being

obsquatulated. He knew what to do about that. He wasn't worried. He simply said to himself: *"Come, my full-up stomach. Come, my full-up stomach, let out all the bees and sting the Sultan's bottom."*

And were those bees angry?
I should say so. And did they
all STING the great and
mighty Sultan's bottom? I should
say so. There was plenty of room
in those capacious pantaloons
for every bee to sting wherever
he wanted. And remember, that
great and mighty Sultan had

# The Rooster's Revenge

a very large, very round bottom, probably the **biggest** bottom the world had ever seen!

Did the great **fat** Sultan jump up and down? I should say so.

Did he screech and yowl and whimper? I should say so.

And did the little red rooster **HOP**

out of those great pantaloons and

fly off safe and sound?

Of course

he did.

cried the Sultan, as he sat with his stinging bottom dunked in a bath of ice-cold water.

"COCKADOODLE-
DOO, MR SULTANA!"
cried the little red rooster. "Now,
will you let me have back my
diamond button?"

"All right, all right," said the
Sultan. "I give in. Anything,
**anything** to get you out
of my sight. Take him up to
my room and give him his
confounded diamond button. It's
in my treasure chest."

So the Sultan's servants
took the little red rooster up

to the Sultan's bedchamber, and gave him the diamond button from out of the Sultan's **TREASURE** chest.

"Now go," they cried. "Fly away! *Shoo!* You've got what you came for. Go, before you get us into any more trouble."

"I'm going. I'm going," replied the little red rooster, the diamond button in his beak. But he was in no hurry to go, for something had caught his eye. He could not **believe** his luck.

The Sultan's "treasure" chest!
The servants had left it open!
So he flew away only as far as
the window-ledge, and he waited
there till all the servants had
left. Then he flew down and
**hopped** across the room and
UP on to the "treasure chest.

Emeralds, rubies, diamonds, pearls, sapphires – the finest jewels in the entire world.

"Ah well. In for a penny, in for a pound," said the little red rooster to himself. "*Come, my empty stomach and gobble down the Sultan's jewels.*"

And that's just what he did.

He gobbled down all the Sultan's jewels, every last one of them.

Then out he flew, out of the window and out over the palace walls, which was not at all easy, because he was rather heavy now. He had to **waddle** all the rest of the way back home, RATTLING as he went.

# The Richest
# Rooster

As he neared the farm, he happened to meet up with his friends again, the **wriggling worms** and the **singing cicadas** and the **burrowing beetles**. So, of course, he just had to tell them all about his great adventures in the Sultan's palace. He was only halfway through his story when the poor old woman, who had been looking high and low for him, spied him at last. She came scuttling along the farm track.

"Where have you been, Little Red Rooster?" she cried. "I've been worried sick."

"Ah, mistress mine," replied

the little red rooster. "Never in your life will you ever have to worry again. And never will we have to go hungry again, either. Look what I have for you."

And he said to himself:

*"Come, my full-up stomach. Come, my full-up stomach and give up all your jewels."*

# The Richest Rooster

Out they poured on to the ground, all of them, all the Sultan's jewels, until there was a great sparkling pile of them at the poor old woman's feet.

Only, she wasn't poor any more, was she?

It took the breath right out of her. She sat down with a **BUMP,** still trying to believe her eyes.

"Goodness me!" she cried. "Goodness me!"

And she *was* good too, goodness itself. Do you know what she did? She gave those jewels to all her poor friends in the countryside round about, just enough for each of them so that no one had too much. She kept for herself all she needed, and no more. But, of course, the little red rooster got to keep his diamond button.

Just you try and take it from him!

**More funny animal stories
from Michael Morpurgo**

# Mudpuddle Farm

**Illustrated by Shoo Rayner**